Hannah Shaw

KU-165-789

BEAR
ON A
BIKE

ALISON GREEN BOOKS

Bear's in the kitchen.

Bear's made a cake.

Bear knocks on Mouse's door.

No! Too late!

Bear on a bike.

Bear on a lorry.

Bear on a bus.

Bear in a trolley.

Bear on
a skateboard.

Bear on a train.

Bear in a canoe.

Bear on
a crane.

Bear on a steam boat.

Bear in a campervan.

Bear in
a tuk-tuk.

Bear in a sedan.

Bear on skis.

Bear in a parachute . . .

Home again!

For Meryn and Wiley

First published in the UK in 2016 by
Alison Green Books
An imprint of Scholastic Children's Books
Euston House, 24 Eversholt Street
London NW1 1DB, UK
A division of Scholastic Ltd
www.scholastic.co.uk
London – New York – Toronto – Sydney – Auckland
Mexico City – New Delhi – Hong Kong

Text & Illustrations copyright © 2016 Hannah Shaw

HB ISBN – 978 1 407 159645
PB ISBN – 978 1 407 159652

All rights reserved.
Printed in Malaysia

1 3 5 7 9 8 6 4 2

The moral rights of Hannah Shaw have been asserted.

Papers used by Scholastic Children's Books
are made from wood grown in sustainable forests.